CO

C000005760

A NEW YORK ADVENTURE

THE NINE LIVES OF GABRIELLE: FOR THREE
SHE PLAYS - BOOK 1

LAURA MARIANI

The
PEOPLE
ALCHEMIST

ABOUT THE AUTHOR

Laura Mariani is an Author, Speaker and Entrepreneur.

She started her consulting business after a successful career as Senior HR Director within global brands in FMCG, Retail, Media and Pharma.

Laura is incredibly passionate about helping other women to break through barriers limiting their personal and/or professional fulfilment. Her best selling nonfiction *STOP IT! It is all in your head* and the *THINK, LOOK & ACT THE PART* series have been described as success and transformation 101.

She is a Fellow of the Chartered Institute of Personnel & Development (FCIPD), Fellow of the Australian Human Resources Institute (FAHRI), Fellow of the Institute of Leadership & Management (FInstLM), Member of the Society of Human Resources Management (SHRM) and Member of the Change Institute.

She is based in London, England with a strong penchant for travel and visiting new places. She is a food lover, ballet fanatic, passionate about music, art, theatre. She likes painting and drawing (for self-expression not selling but hey, you never know…), tennis, rugby, and of course fashion (the Pope is Catholic after all).

www.thepeoplealchemist.com
@PeopleAlchemist
instagram.com/lauramariani_author

NEW FICTION BY LAURA MARIANI

www.thepeoplealchemist.com
@PeopleAlchemist
instagram.com/lauramariani_author

NEW FICTION BY LAURA MARIANI

THE NINE LIVES OF GABRIELLE:
FOR THREE SHE PLAYS - BOOK 2

SEARCHING FOR
Goren

LAURA MARIANI

GABRIELLE STORY CONTINUE ...

NEW NON-FICTION BY LAURA MARIANI

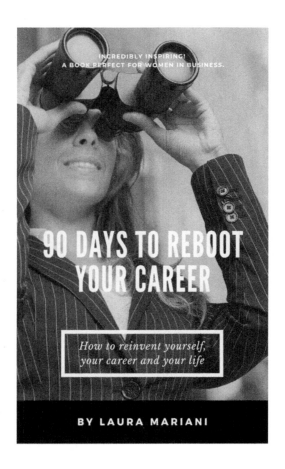

Non-Fiction

STOP IT! It is all in your head

The RULE BOOK to Smash The infamous glass ceiling - For women & young women everywhere - personal transformation & success 101.

The Think, Look & Act The Part Series.

Think The Part

Upgrade your consciousness and mind-set. Make winning a key part of your life and business.

Look The Part

Upgrade your personal brand. Make presenting your unique Best Self a key part of your life and business.

Act The Part

A personal coach to act in spite of fear, right here, right now.

More non-fiction books and courses are coming soon. For new releases, giveaways and pre-release specials check www.thepeoplealchemist.com

You can also buy my books and courses directly from me at www.payhip.com/LauraMariani

"YOU'RE ONLY HERE NOW;
YOU'RE ONLY ALIVE IN THIS MOMENT"
- JON KABAT-ZINN

To New York, one of my three loves

A NEW YORK ADVENTURE

G abrielle was getting ready to go out.
A surprise from Mr Wonderful.

Out for dinner and then to the Opera. Going out again felt incredible after almost two years of off and on lockdowns. They were celebrating the day that they met. He was always full of surprises: spontaneous, romantic and thoughtful.

She hadn't had the time to think carefully about what to wear and was getting ready at the last minute. She decided on wearing the same dress she wore when they met: the white dress culpable for so many mischiefs, the dress that started it all.

Albeit it was so lovely to go out again now that all the restrictions had been lifted, it was also so strange seeing a mix-match of people with and without masks everywhere you went. The anxiety and slight fear when hearing someone coughing. You can just see the suspicion on people's faces. "Has he/she got IT?" The new dreaded C-word.

However, slowly and surely, life is getting back to normality. Time is passing by, and life needs to go on. She missed travelling and going out. Socialising and the theatre, she loved the theatre, and Mr Wonderful knew her well.

BANG! Ouch...

The collision was surprisingly strong, considering they were both just walking. Gabrielle had lost her balance, but he was quick and promptly grabbed her by the waist to keep her from falling. Unfortunately, her coffee wasn't that lucky and splattered everywhere.

. . .

E-V-E-R-Y-W-H-E-R-E on her white dress.

Memories. The smell of coffee and cologne. He smelled real good. Affirmations were still playing in her ears when they banged into each other.

"I am a Goddess; I am a Queen"
- very empowering, perhaps a tad scary for a man to hear when they first meet you.

"I am so so sorry," he said.

"Gosh, thank you, Jesus, he is so handsome,"
Gabrielle thought as she looked up at the piercing blue eyes, the dazzling smile peaking through the mask now half down his chin.

Gabrielle felts like he was looking straight into her soul. He was genuinely mortified by what had happened.

"I'm OK, thank you. Not a big deal, really. It is only coffee," she said, playing it cool.

He didn't stop looking straight into her eyes, not even for a second. She didn't know if to back up to keep some parvence of social distancing (and decor) or hold the stare. Fuck it. Hold it.

She felt like getting closer instead. She didn't. He offered to get her dress dry-cleaned for her. Gabrielle wondered if he was living in London or if he got stuck here when lockdown started. He had that distinctive North American, New York accent.

"Please, let me do this for you. I live just around the corner: if the dry-cleaners are closed, I can wash your dress and have it ready in a couple of hours. Perhaps even make you a coffee while you wait. One that you can drink this time,"
    he insisted.

"Wait, did he just ask me back to his place and offer to wash my dress?" pondering,
    "This is the type of exchange you see in Hallmark movies. Or the real crime police dramas".

She squinted with her deep dark eyes staring into his and said:

"Is this a cheap ploy to see me naked?"

"No, no, no, YES "
    ... mortified
    "No, no. I mean would be great but no".

· · ·

She smiled profusely and felt like teasing him.

"I feel like I'm in a scene from the Vicar of Dibley: where is the camera?"

"What?"
looking puzzled and obviously not getting the reference.

"Sorry, British cultural reference. I'm kidding. I'm OK, seriously, no need to go through that much trouble. It is only coffee".

And then he asked her for a date. Gabrielle remembered how she quickly glanced at his hands to see if there was any appearance of a wedding ring. Both hands, to be sure. And no, there was no ring or any signs that he was wearing one regularly either.

He offered to cook too.

"What about social distancing?"
Gabrielle said.

"I think we broke that rule already. We can eat outside if that makes you feel any better or safer,"
he said.

"I don't know you".

"I'm trying to remedy that",

and sensing her reluctance
"Can I have at least your number?"

Gabrielle was intrigued and attracted to him, so she gave him her number. He had just finished tapping her number into his mobile when her phone started ringing in her pocket.

"Are you going to get that?" He asked.

"Pardon?"

"Your phone, are you going to answer it?"

"No, it's rude; I am talking to you. I can see who called me later".

"It's me".

"You can't be missing me already; I'm still here,"
    Gabrielle said (he is keen, a good sign).

"I just want to make sure I have the right number. And you now have mine too"
    he was grinning too.
    "Are you sure I cannot convince you to have dinner with me tonight?"

. . .

"Not tonight".

"Another night then. Tomorrow?"

He was sure of himself without being arrogant and persistent. He knew exactly what he wanted and was going for it.

Gabrielle felt really good about the encounter and excited as she hadn't been for a long time. She remembered waving and walking away. Actually, she had never felt like this before. Her body was on fire, her spirit soaring, and she was walking on clouds.

It would have been the perfect exit had she not turned around to see if he was still there. But she couldn't help herself. She had to.

He was still there, standing still, looking. Smiling.

As she turned around the corner, her phone vibrated, a text:

"Now, I am missing you."
    "that's understandable", she replied.

Just like that, that day, everything changed. He was everything she always wanted but wasn't quite ready for before. And it was still going.

. . .

"Honey, are you almost ready?"

Mr Wonderful asked, peeking through the bedroom door, "the Uber will be here in the next few minutes".

"Where are we going exactly now?"

as it was too early for the Opera.

"Dinner".

"I know, you said. Where though?"

Gabrielle, the in-control planner, needed to know.

"I made a reservation for Balthazar in Covent Garden".

Nice, and walking distance to the Royal Opera House. She had mentioned to him that she had been in New York; he must have remembered.

Balthazar was busy. Very.

They were greeted as the walked in and taken straight to their table. The relatively small room, with faux-nicotine-stained walls, a station clock, and the poised amber hue, is almost made for Instagram.

There was a lively buzz in the air.

Just as well, Mr Wonderful had made a reservation because there was a queue outside waiting to be seated, and many who tried a walk-in turned away, disappointed with the wait.

. . .

Gabrielle ordered the mussels for the starter and steak tartare for the main course. Mr Wonderful had ordered champagne seemingly on tap to wash everything down.

He was soo good at remembering all the little details and celebrating every occasion, no matter how small or big. Anything she ever said, he listened and acted upon. She was speechless actually that he remembered so much about everything that she told him.

He was spontaneous, romantic, thoughtful, and passionate with piercing blue eyes. No wonder she called him Mr Wonderful.

They were seated in the right-hand corner of the restaurant, just in front of the bar with a good view of the room and the window, great for people-watching, should you want to.

They could barely hear each other lost amongst the live jazz, the chitchat and the noise of plates and cutlery, but, at the same time, it was very intimate and cosy. Even in the middle of a crowd, Mr Wonderful only had eyes for her.

Chitchat, chitchat.

The same sounds, different vibe.

Clink clink … clink …

. . .

Gabrielle adored grand set-piece spectacular restaurants with ambience, and Balthazar is undoubtedly that and perhaps, one of the best brasseries in London for its atmosphere, happy, friendly staff and service, living up to the reputation of his New York City original.

The first time she had visited Balthazar in New York was on the weekend for brunch, steak and eggs, New York pancakes and Balthazar Bloody Mary.

The VP took her there. They had only just met a few days earlier.

skahdeedath bideedoodop… gahdugat …

"NYC Balthazar is much bigger than this one", was going through her head.

It was in the midst of the full Sex and The City hype at that time. A place everyone wanted to be seen at.

And the VP made sure they had the most visible table in the room.

He was waving at people, smiling.

"You see that man on the corner?"

Gabrielle turned her head slightly to see what he was talking about.

. . .

"He is the CEO of such and such .... Major client".

"That one over there is the anchor of NBC News",
     name dropping
     "and that blonde woman over there is in a famous soap opera".

People watching. Or, even more important, been watched. They were seated bang in the middle of the room, which was definitely good for that. Not a great table to have a conversation and get to know someone.

     Then again, Gabrielle didn't think that's why they were there.

That was the first date with the VP after Gabrielle arrived in New York.

The trip was a last-minute decision after a long-term relationship break-up.
     Another failed relationship.

Gabrielle had reached boiling point and felt claustrophobic. She needed to escape, an adventure, re-group and re-think what she would do. She felt like she had thrown five years down the drain. She had given everything she could and had nothing more to offer right now.

"Let's get married and have babies,"

he said out of the blue, after five years and all the previous talk about a commitment that went nowhere.

Unbelievable. Too little, too late.

Mentally she had moved on. She wasn't sure anymore if she saw a future with him. Growing old with him. Or as the father of her children.

Her friends always told her,

"Why don't you get pregnant?

You know, a-c-c-i-d-e-n-t-a-l-l-y. Things happen all the time, and you'll at least have a child".

Gabrielle knew that some (many? few?) women do that, and sometimes it works well. Sometimes not so much.

But she, she could never bring herself to do it. To even try.

There are enough unwanted children in the world, and bringing another potential unwanted one in didn't feel like an option to her. Although to be fair, she was always planning for her career, move after move, and it never quite seemed to be the right time to get pregnant.

Moving town, travelling, and a new bigger job always sounded more like desirable and viable options.

Perhaps she didn't want a child.

The idea of a child, yes. The idea of being a mother, yes.

Doing it not so much. She had thought if having children was so ingrained that she had to want it, being a mother as the pinnacle of being a woman. She always wanted to be free.

Always wanted to travel, free to do what she wanted, when she wanted.

Marriage too.

The idea of an all-encompassing, consuming, can't live without someone love affair was thrilling. A strong man to look after her. Finding a man she could bear 24/7 without feeling trapped, not so much. And now, all she wanted was to take off.

Just go somewhere.

New York - the Big Apple dream - had always been lurking in the background. This was the perfect opportunity to take the plunge. So she wrote to her boss requesting time off and got her tickets. Three months in New York, a mini-sabbatical. Longer than a holiday but short enough not to need a working visa.

On her taxi ride to the airport, she felt like Indiana Jones

(ok, mini Indiana Jones); it was her first-ever trip alone, non-work-related.

Not visiting anybody. Nothing planned. Just her and New York.

Exhilarating and scary AF.

The flight felt much longer than she imagined, maybe because she had to squeeze between two enormous individuals overflowing into her seat. Perhaps because they never stopped moving, talking, eating. ALL the way throughout the flight.

"Jesus, what's wrong with actually keeping quiet for a few hours. Or just sleep",

she asked herself, already knowing the answer. To Gabrielle, it felt like people are afraid of silence, and they need desperately to fill in.

"God knows what they are afraid will happen if they are alone with their thoughts. So most of the time, people fill the void with absolute total nonsense. And unfortunately, on a plane, there isn't much of an escape route. You have to listen. Well, kind of".

Chitchat, chitchat, blah blah blah...

And constant eating.

"Really? Who brings snacks on a long haul flight? I'm sure starvation will not sneak up on you if you don't constantly munch on something. Out loud. The airline already provides food, starvation prevented".

Note to self: MUST book business class for the return flight.

As the plane landed at JFK, people proceeded calmly out of the aircraft, following the different signs directing toward

Customs and Border Protection. Brits are good at queuing, and it comes naturally. Whilst the passengers were arriving near the actual desks, Gabrielle was jilted out of her thoughts:

"Ma'am, step behind the yellow line".

"Is she talking to me?"
Gabrielle thought. "Did she just call me Ma'am?"

She didn't know if she was more upset about being called Ma'am ("do I look that old?"), especially as the officer didn't look that much younger herself or being shouted at by an overbearing sturdy officer WITH A GUN.

Apparently, she was doing something wrong. Gabrielle didn't know what it was, but it seemed to have annoyed her. A lot.
The Border Protection officer got closer to Gabrielle, far too close for comfort because she was sure they weren't about to *faire la bise* and proceeded to shout, again, explaining
("I must have looked really tick", she wondered),

"Ma'am, step behind the yellow line. You have not been admitted into the United States until you have gone through my colleague at the desk. Step behind the yellow line."

"What? Really? I'm pretty sure the plane landed at JFK, and I'm pretty sure JFK happens to be in the US of A. So what is she going to do? Throw me back into the sea?"

• • •

As all these thoughts were going through her mind, Gabrielle sheepishly said,

" Sure, no problem, officer"

she didn't feel that courageous to argue with an armed, angry person in authority.

The reputation of trigger-happy American police (whatever) is infamous and, unfortunately, or fortunately, was imprinted in her mind. She also had images of being locked up with no contact with the external world and sent back. Or kept somewhere.

God knows where.

"I have watched too many police movies,"
Gabrielle thought.

What a contrast from the officer behind the desk.

He was a young male in his late twenties or early thirties, seemingly shy. And he was unlucky enough to have three ladies who had just landed from Manchester at his desk. They were having a great time, which seemed to have started on their plane, or before, with copious alcohol. One might say they were "tipsy".

And determined to have a good time.

New York was their stop for the night before embarking on a Caribbean cruise, and they were officially on holiday, prob-ably FROM Manchester. They must have been in their late fifties, early sixties, or at least what looked like sixty or thereabout in Gabrielle's mind. They were making all sorts of advances to the poor guy who, by now, had become red-faced up to his roots.

And was getting redder by the minute.

They were totally shameless, and who can blame them? He was cute, wearing a uniform (always helps) and reinforced by each other and vodka martinis.

He couldn't wait to get them off his desk soon enough.

Bless.

Then came her turn. Gabrielle was sure she had never been asked that many questions going through any other customs in any other country. At least she couldn't remember. Neither did she think they sounded like legitimate questions (to grant entry into the country).

Perhaps he was reasserting his authority and regaining control after the cruise ladies, or maybe that's what he usually asked. Who knows.

Gabrielle preferred to think there was some mild flirtation going on. But, hey, he was cute, and it was a friendly welcome to New York. She felt smug and almost tempted to turn back and poke her tongue out at the

"Step behind the yellow line" officer but thought perhaps better not.

. . .

She stepped out of the airport and looked for the taxi lane.

"324 West 44th Street, please. The TownePlace Suite Manhattan, please"
    let the adventure begin.

As they were driving toward the city, the taxi driver made small talk. Gabrielle was distracted: she was soaking in the atmosphere, excited about what the next three months would bring.

She had chosen an extended-stay boutique-style hotel right in the heartbeat of NYC's Times Square and within walking distance to Broadway, Restaurant Row, Macy's Herald Square, Empire State Building and many other famous attractions.
    She wanted to have the most authentic experience possible in a neighbourhood-style accommodation with a kitchenette.

Of course, New York is full of places to eat everywhere, and she could easily go out for dinner if she wanted to. However, she both liked the convenience and pretending she was living there, if only for a little bit.
    Perhaps cook a few meals from time to time.

Come to think of it, Gabrielle had never been out for dinner or in a pub by herself.

. . .

E-V-E-R.

Even when meeting people, she always checked to ensure they arrived first.

"Baby steps Gabri, baby steps,"
    she said to herself.

She flew in early in the morning to enjoy almost a full first day and then crash at "normal" sleeping time to beat the jet lag. She arrived at the hotel around 2 pm and, after a quick shower and change of clothes, she was ready to start exploring.

Gabrielle had bought an Insight New York City Pocket Map that she had studied on the plane and planned a few days out.

"I know it's an adventure, but some structure won't go amiss".
    She had been trying to decipher the New York street system …

"Odd-numbered streets go west, and even-numbered streets go east. Right, ok …. And odd-numbered buildings are on the north side of the street, and even-numbered addresses are on the south. So streets run east to west, and avenues run north to south. I think I got it".

. . .

She ventured to Time Square, then the New York Public Library on Fifth Avenue and then a little spontaneous wander for her first outing.

Everything was so new and yet so familiar. She recognised buildings and streets at almost every other turn.

Hello there, she thought as a handsome guy was walking by, going in the opposite direction.

"Talk to self; you just arrived, Gabri. Give it time".

As they crossed each other paths, the stranger smiled at her, a dazzling smile. He wasn't her usual type. She usually liked the tall, dark, handsome ones (or blonde) but definitely tall. She was 5.5ish and liked wearing heels.

He was more of an average height, a.k.a. shorter, with a soap opera-ish all American look.

"Nice shoes", he said.
Interesting pick-up line.

"Pardon?"
Gabrielle replied.

"You look like you're walking with purpose. Are you going somewhere specific?"

. . .

She didn't want to give too much away; he was a perfect stranger after all. He could be Jack The Ripper or Ted Bunty for all she knew. And before she could answer,

"I'm on my way to the office for a meeting. Here is my card with my cell and office extension. Can I meet you for a drink later on?"

Mmmmmh …

"Or perhaps a coffee tomorrow morning?"
    he said as she looked pensive.

Ok, that sounded more reasonable. Gabrielle was still hesitating.

"You can come into the building where I work and ask for me, and then we can go for a coffee?".
    Better. Definitely better.

"Let's say 10 am? How does that sound?".

"Sounds like a plan", she replied.

"And what is your name, lovely lady?"

• • •

"Gabrielle".

"Nice to meet you, Gabrielle. I'll see you tomorrow. Bye".

VP OF CORPORATE FINANCE - said the business card. VP uh? Not a bad start for an adventure.

The second morning she had the American breakfast at the hotel; she wasn't quite used to having breakfast in the morning, but she thought it was better to have one considering she had planned a long day out walking—eggs, bacon, sausage and pancakes.

She had contemplated all night if to go and meet the VP.

"What have I got to lose? It's just coffee and a chat in a public space. What's the worse that can happen?".

His office was in a massive building (aren't they all) in MidTown Manhattan by the Rockefeller Center. The reception buzzed his office extension to let him know Gabrielle was there.

"You look lovely today,"
   he said. He smelled of fresh cologne and had a crisp blue striped shirt, making his eyes stand out.

· · ·

"Let's go. It is only a few minutes away, right down the steps from 1 Rockefeller Plaza. There is a nice coffee bar with espressos and very nice coffee in general. You'll like it".

He was very talkative and wanted to know more about Gabrielle. Not too much, but more. The VP was making plans for the weekend. Brunch at Balthazar.

We can do this. We can do that. Plans for the two of them.

A bit presumptuous.

Mind, it was her first weekend in New York, and she quite liked the idea of having some company. The fact that she was there for a limited amount of time made it more appealing.

Probably to both of them.

Time flew quickly. He had to go back to the office, and they agreed to meet outside Balthazar. Gabrielle had plans to walk some more and had studied her map. She was so proud when someone who looked like a tourist asked her for directions.

"Success".

Everything was going so well until she reached the West Village, and then it went Pete Tong,

"What happened here?"

. . .

The familiar grid-like street system was nowhere to see. As she walked around, she stumbled on the Magnolia Bakery. She got a couple of cupcakes to see what the fuss was about.

Gabrielle tried to look for familiar landmarks and streets to get back to the hotel.

"I'd be damned if I get out the map",
	she said to herself. She could have easily reached for a taxi, but she wanted to walk. Needed to walk.

She arrived back at the hotel exhausted and went straight to bed. Day two was over by 8 pm—rock'n roll, baby.

She woke up in the morning and took the time to savour her coffee and enjoy the New York view, still not believing she was actually here.

"Time to get ready for brunch".
	That day was the beginning of her affair with the VP.

He became her chaperon with benefits. He knew how to live and have fun. The high New York life.

Their relationship grew into a whirlwind, inhibited affair.
	She felt like she was in a movie that, one day, was going to end inevitably—all more exciting for it.

· · ·

Theatres. Cinemas. Museums.

Gabrielle got to know the most famous spots in New York. And got to have sex there too.

The VP bought her a lot of gifts. Perfume. Flowers. Jewellery. Money was his "love" language. Lots of lingerie. He loved Victoria's Secrets. She had to clear a drawer just for it.

He was the perfect chaperon and was not shy in introducing her to his acquaintances.

"This is Gabrielle, my *friend* visiting from London, England", he would introduce her.

The VP took her to his place in the Hamptons too. He had a house in Cooper's Beach.

Gabrielle had heard of the Hamptons: the group of towns, and villages on the eastern end of Long Island in New York state, a popular getaway for people from New York City.

When the VP told her the Hamptons were in New York, she was perplexed. It took them about two-and-a-half hours by car to get to Westhampton, where the Hamptons start.

Two-and-half-hours!

· · ·

And to reach the end of the island's South Fork is another 50 miles east.

It's like saying Manchester is in London.

"Perspective, Gabrielle, everything is a matter of perspective", she thought.

Gabrielle could see why so many of the wealthy and famous spend their summers here: ocean breezes, white sand beaches, excellent seafood, lively parties, and the rural atmosphere of Long Island's South Fork and the more laid-back Southampton Town.

For the weekend, the VP had planned a visit to the Shinnecock Golf Club, one of the historic golfing institutions in the United States apparently.

Even though it has been renovated and expanded, its character remains substantially the same as a century ago. An accompanying member must sign in all guests;

obviously, the VP was a member. He also bought her the appropriate golf attire and briefed her on the Club's strict rules.

"Hello, are you there? Honey?"

Mr Wonderful said.

"You seem miles away. Are you ok?"

. . .

Gabrielle was yanked back into present London.

"Yes, yes, I was just enjoying the food and lost in my thoughts",

"I hope he hasn't been talking about something important, and I missed it", she thought.

They finished their pre-theatre dinner and strolled toward the Royal Opera House around the corner. Hand in hand. Like the day they met, the electricity between was palpable. Was it too good to be true? Sometimes she doubted she deserved him/it.

They were going to see Madame Butterfly, the fascinating and heartbreaking story of words and promises carelessly spoken with inevitable consequences.

Un bel dì, vedremo
Levarsi un fil di fumo
Sull'estremo confin del mare
E poi la nave appare
Poi la nave bianca …..

The VP had taken Gabrielle to the Metropolitan to see Madame Butterfly. Because he loved Opera, better still, be seen at the Opera, the best seats of course.

• • •

"I love this aria",
    he said.

It is incredible how the same experience can differ at different times. The music transported her in and out of her body, back and forward in time.

....Entra nel porto
Romba il suo saluto
Vedi? È venuto!
Io non gli scendo incontro, io no
Mi metto là sul ciglio del colle e aspetto
E aspetto gran tempo
E non mi pesa
La lunga attesa

Mr Wonderful looked at Gabrielle and kissed her gently on her forehead,
    "Io sono qui, e non mi pesa la lunga attesa. Io ti aspetto".

DISCLAIMER

A New York Adventure is a work of fiction.

Although its form is that of travelogue/semi-autobiography it is not one.

With the exception of public places, any resemblance to persons living or dead is coincidental. Space and time have been rearranged to suit the convenience of the book, memory has its own story to tell.

The opinions expressed are those of the characters and should not be confused with the author's.

AUTHOR'S NOTE

Thank you so much for reading *A New York Adventure*.

I hope you enjoyed this novella as an escapist story, but perhaps you also glimpsed something beneath as you read. A review would be much appreciated as it helps other readers discover the story. Thanks.

If you sign up for my newsletter you'll be notified of giveaways, new releases and receive personal updates from behind the scenes of my business and books.

Go to www.thepeoplealchemist.com to get started.

Places in the book

I have set the story in real places in London and New York - find out more about them or perhaps, go and visit:

- Balthazar, London
- Balthazar, New York
- Blue Bottle Coffee
- Covent Garden
- Empire State Building

- Magnolia Bakery
- Rockefeller Center
- Royal Opera House, London
- The New York Public Library
- The Metropolitan Opera, New York
- The Shinnecock Golf Club
- Times Square
- TownePlace Suites, Manhattan/Times Square
- NYC West Village

Bibliography

I read a lot of books as part of my research. Some of them together with other references include:

Psycho-Cybernetics - **Maxwell Maltz**
The Complete Reader - **Neville Goddard**

The Vicar of Dibley - British sitcom starring Dawn French as the Vicar of the rural parish of Dibley, It made its debut in 1994.

The **"Bermondsey Goes Balearic"** article in the late 1987 by Paul Oakenfold for Terry Farley and Pete Heller's Boys Own fanzine (*it's all gone Pete Tong*).

Madama Butterfly is an opera in three acts by Giacomo Puccini, with an Italian libretto by Luigi Illica and Giuseppe Giacosa, premiered at La Scala, in Milan in 1904.